Dear Parents:

Congratulations! Your child is taking the first steps on an exciting journey. The destination? Independent reading!

STEP INTO READING® will help your child get there. The program offers five steps to reading success. Each step includes fun stories and colorful art or photographs. In addition to original fiction and books with favorite characters, there are Step into Reading Non-Fiction Readers, Phonics Readers and Boxed Sets, Sticker Readers, and Comic Readers—a complete literacy program with something to interest every child.

Learning to Read, Step by Step!

Ready to Read Preschool–Kindergarten
• big type and easy words • rhyme and rhythm • picture clues
For children who know the alphabet and are eager to begin reading.

Reading with Help Preschool–Grade 1
• basic vocabulary • short sentences • simple stories
For children who recognize familiar words and sound out new words with help.

Reading on Your Own Grades 1–3
• engaging characters • easy-to-follow plots • popular topics
For children who are ready to read on their own.

Reading Paragraphs Grades 2–3
• challenging vocabulary • short paragraphs • exciting stories
For newly independent readers who read simple sentences with confidence.

Ready for Chapters Grades 2–4
• chapters • longer paragraphs • full-color art
For children who want to take the plunge into chapter books but still like colorful pictures.

STEP INTO READING® is designed to give every child a successful reading experience. The grade levels are only guides; children will progress through the steps at their own speed, developing confidence in their reading.

Remember, a lifetime love of reading starts with a single step!

Special thanks to Alex Wiltshire, Sherin Kwan, Jay Castello, Kelsey Ranallo, and Milo Bengtsson

Visit us on the Web!
rhcbooks.com
minecraft.net

Educators and librarians, for a variety of teaching tools, visit us at RHTeachersLibrarians.com

ISBN 978-0-593-70946-7 (trade) — ISBN 978-0-593-70947-4 (lib. bdg.)
ISBN 978-0-593-70948-1 (ebook)

Printed in the United States of America
10 9 8 7 6 5 4 3 2 1

MINECRAFT

MOBS IN THE MANSION!

by Arie Kaplan

illustrated by Alan Batson

Random House 🏠 New York

Emmy and Birch
were mining
deep in the caves.
Emmy collected
three diamonds
and put them
in her inventory.

"Let's craft
a diamond pickaxe,"
Emmy said.
"We could use it
to mine *anything*!"

Byte pointed his nose

at a dark oak tree

and barked.

"Good point, Byte."

Emmy nodded.

"We need wood

to craft the pickaxe!"

"Coming right up!"

Birch said.

He punched the tree.

It broke apart

into blocks of wood.

8

Emmy turned the blocks
into oak planks and sticks.
She used the planks
to create a crafting table.
"Now we can craft
the diamond pickaxe!"
she said.

Birch looked around.
There were
dark oak trees everywhere.
Their leaves were like
a giant green roof
covering the explorers.

"I think we've wandered
into a dark forest!" Birch said.
"Let's go exploring,"
Emmy said.
Maybe they could gather
some useful materials in there!

11

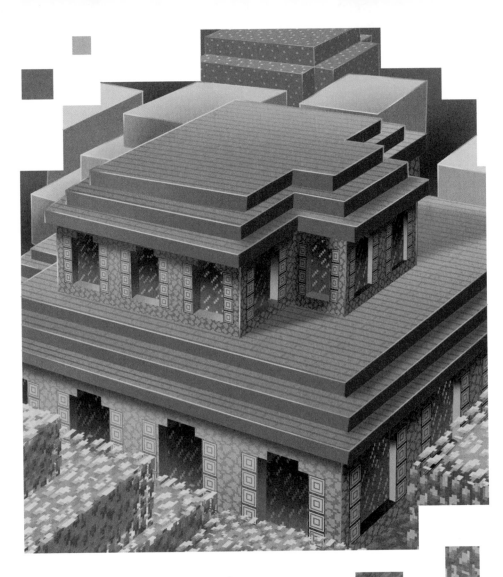

Soon they spotted
a strange wooden building.

It was a woodland mansion.

The massive structure
poked through the trees.

The building looked scary,
but Emmy and Birch
couldn't resist
stepping inside.

On the first floor, the hallways
were long and winding.
The red carpet on the floor
looked so fancy.
But on the second floor,
they ran into an evoker!

The evoker conjured three vexes.
The little flying mobs
wielded iron swords.
They flew down the hall
at top speed!

Emmy swatted at the vexes.

Byte chased them.

Soon the vexes were defeated!

But the evoker
was still there!
Birch swung
the diamond pickaxe.
Just then, the evoker
summoned a fang attack!
A line of fangs came
for Emmy, Birch, and Byte!
They jumped just in time!

17

"We've got to make a break for it," Emmy decided. "Let's search every inch of this mansion for something that will help us battle that evoker."

Birch nodded.
The three friends fought
their way out of the hall
and kept going.

19

When they saw a jail cell,

Emmy opened the door.

There was an allay inside,

but there was also a vindicator!

The vindicator lunged at Birch
with their iron axe.
Birch fought bravely,
but the pickaxe wasn't as good
to use in battle as a sword.
He couldn't defeat the illager,
so the buddies ran away
as fast as they could.

The vindicator was behind them,
and they weren't alone.
The evoker had caught up
to them, too!

Emmy and Birch needed to escape,

but there was a big, wide wall

in their way.

Birch had a plan.

While he distracted the illagers,

Emmy would mine her way

through the wall.

It was a good plan!

Using the pickaxe,

Emmy hacked away at the wall.

Behind it was a secret room!

Emmy and Byte entered the room.

Inside, Emmy found

a clump of obsidian.

Emmy used the diamond pickaxe
to mine the obsidian.
"This pickaxe didn't seem
very useful before," she said.
"But without it,
I couldn't do this!"

There was a block of diamond
inside the obsidian.
Emmy used her crafting table
to break the diamond block
into little diamonds.

Then she used those diamonds
to craft diamond swords
for herself and Birch!

The swords would finally
protect them
against the illagers.

The vindicator and evoker
charged at them.
Emmy hit the vindicator
with her new sword.
Birch swung his sword
at the evoker.

Both illagers were defeated.

As the evoker fell in battle,

they dropped

a totem of undying.

Birch picked it up.

When Emmy, Birch, Byte,

and the allay

left the woodland mansion,

Birch was tired from the battle.

Because of that,

he wasn't looking

where he was going . . .

and he walked off a cliff!

Luckily, Birch was holding on to the totem of undying and was unharmed. *Whew!* That was close!

To celebrate their victory
over the illagers,
the friends had a picnic
in the meadow.

The allay
even brought them food.
It was a perfect way
to end the day!